DATE DUE

Sail Away

For Bridget and Jessica with love.
F.M.

For Jim and J.J., my brother's good friends.
D.M.

Sail Away

Florence McNeil & David McPhail

ORCA BOOK PUBLISHERS

AFTER YOU
scrape the bottom

paint the hull

polish the brightwork

varnish the spars

mend the sails

and launch the craft ...

YOU
step the mast

rig the stays

bail the bilge

batten the   hatches

bend the sails

thread the fairleads

hoist the halyards

trim the sheets

vang the boom

weigh the anchor

take the wheel

heave a sigh

and sail away.

Sailor Talk

scrape the bottom — clean the old paint and barnacles off the bottom

paint the hull — paint the outer body of the boat

swab the decks — wash the floor of the boat

polish the brightwork — shine the metal and wood trim

varnish the spars — put clear paint on the mast

mend the sails — sew up torn sails

launch the craft — put the boat in the water

step the mast — put the mast in its holder so it stands up

rig the stays — put on the ropes that keep the mast from falling forwards or backwards

tighten the shrouds — tighten the ropes that keep the mast from falling sideways

bail the bilge — take all the water out of the inside of the boat

batten the hatches — tie down all the loose doors to the inside of the boat

bend the sails — tie the sails onto the mast

thread the fairleads — put the ropes through the metal holes that keep them from getting tangled

hoist the halyards — pull the rope that lifts the sails up the mast

trim the sheets — tighten the ropes that hold the bottom of the sails in the right place

vang the boom — tighten another rope that holds the bottom of the big sail

weigh the anchor — pull the anchor out of the water

take the wheel — hold the wheel that steers the boat

heave a sigh — whew! It's all done

and sail away — off you go!

Canadian Cataloguing in Publication Data
McNeil, Florence.
Sail away

ISBN 1-55143-147-5

1. Sailing—juvenile literature. I. McPhail, David, 1940–
II. Title.
GV8111.N36 2000   j797.1'24   C00-910393-7

Library of Congress Catalog Card Number: 00-102428

Orca Book Publishers gratefully acknowledges the
support for our publishing programs provided by the
following agencies: The Government of Canada through
the Book Publishing Industry Development Program
(BPIDP), The Canada Council for the Arts, and the
British Columbia Arts Council.

Design by Christine Toller
Printed and bound in Canada

IN CANADA   **IN THE UNITED STATES**
Orca Book Publishers   **Orca Book Publishers**
PO Box 5626, Station B   PO Box 468
Victoria, BC Canada   Custer, WA USA
V8R 6S4   98240-0468

02 01 00   5 4 3 2 1